SUPERMAN

IS A
GOOD CITIZEN

Written By
CHRISTOPHER HARBO

Illustrated by
OTIS FRAMPTON

SUPERMAN created by
Jerry Siegel and Joe Shuster
by special arrangement with the
Jerry Siegel Family

Capstone Young Readers
a capstone imprint

Superman is a good citizen. He works to make his community better. The people of Metropolis can rely on him to protect their city.

When a robbery gets foiled, Superman returns all of the stolen loot.

The Man of Steel is a good citizen because he is honest and obeys the law.

When disaster strikes Metropolis, Superman pitches in to pick up the pieces.

The Man of Steel is a good citizen because
he helps clean up his city.

When buildings are ablaze, Superman works with firefighters to put out the flames.

Superman is a good citizen because he cooperates with community helpers.

When people are in danger, Superman carries them to safety.

Superman is a good citizen because he protects others from harm.

When Metropolis makes the news, Superman finds a way to learn more.

Superman is a good citizen because he stays informed.

When there's trouble next door, Superman gladly helps out.

Superman is a good citizen because he's also a good neighbor.

When Metropolis has a problem, Superman offers to solve it.

The Man of Steel is a good citizen because he volunteers his time and talents.

When officers lend him a hand, Superman thanks them for their help.

Superman is a good citizen because he respects the police.

Whenever super-villains strike, Superman always swoops in to save the day.

He keeps the good citizens of Metropolis safe
from the bad!

SUPERMAN SAYS...

- Being a good citizen means obeying the law, like when I return the stolen gold to the bank instead of keeping it for myself.

- Being a good citizen means making your community better, like when I help clean up the city after a battle with Bizarro.

- Being a good citizen means being a good neighbor, like when I help a polar bear family by saving their cub.

- Being a good citizen means respecting the police, like when I thank the officer for helping me capture Toyman.

- Being a good citizen means being the best you that you can be!

BE YOUR BEST
with the World's Greatest Super Heroes!

ONLY FROM CAPSTONE!

DC Super Heroes Character Education
is published by Capstone Young Readers
A Capstone Imprint
1710 Roe Crest Drive
North Mankato, Minnesota 56003
www.mycapstone.com

STAR40357

Editor: Julie Gassman
Designer: Hilary Wacholz
Art Director: Bob Lentz

Cataloging-in-Publication Data is available
at the Library of Congress website.

ISBN: 978-1-62370-956-3

Printed and bound in the USA.
010848S18